S0-APP-265

A Curious George® Activity Book

I Am Curious About Me

Featuring Margret and H. A. Rey's Curious George

SCHOLASTIC INC.

New York   Toronto   London   Auckland   Sydney

Activities by Jan Carr

Illustrations by Manny Campana

No part of this publication may be reproduced in whole or in
part, or stored in a retrieval system, or transmitted in any
form or by any means, electronic, mechanical, photocoyping,
recording, or otherwise, without written permission of the
publisher. For information regarding permission, write to
Scholastic Inc., 730 Broadway, New York, NY 10003.

ISBN 0-590-44032-2

Copyright © 1990 by Scholastic Inc.
All rights reserved. Published by Scholastic Inc.

12 11 10 9 8 7 6 5 4 3   2 3 4 5/9

Printed in the U.S.A.   08

First Scholastic printing, November 1990

This is George.
He lives with the man
with the yellow hat.

George is very curious.
He is curious about you.
Write your name here.

_____

If you are curious about the answers to the
puzzles, look in the back of the book.
Not all of the pages have right answers.
Some of the pages are just about you.

In this book, George goes to school
and learns some things about himself.
You can learn some things about yourself, too.
To start, solve the puzzle below.

It was open house at George's school,
so the man with the yellow hat
had come to school with George.
You can travel from your house to school also.
Follow this maze. Only one path is right.
Draw a picture of your house next to the word *start*.
Draw a picture of your school next to the word *finish*.

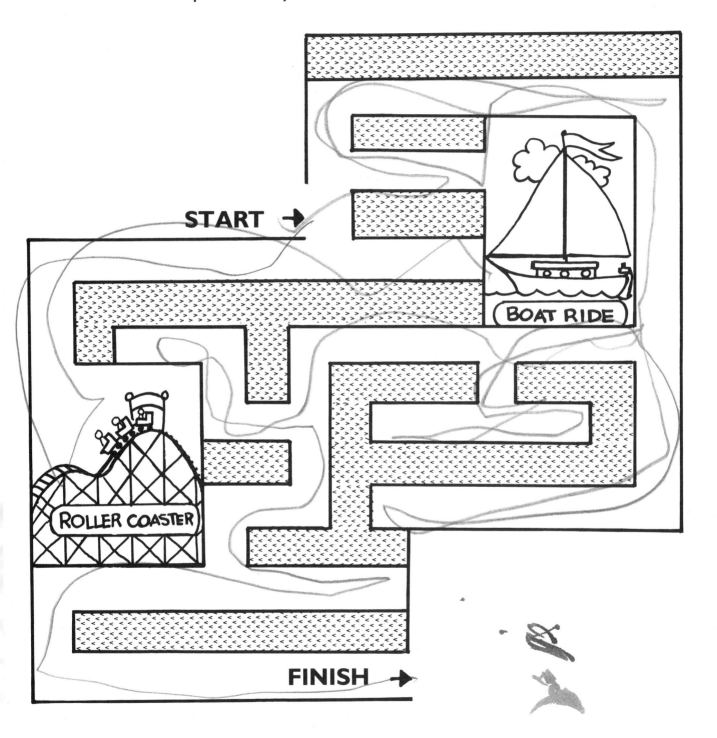

START →

BOAT RIDE

ROLLER COASTER

FINISH →

Different people live in different kinds of houses.
Each of the children below knows his or her address.
Draw a line connecting each child with the right house.

39 Maple Lane

679 River Road

218 Bloomfield Street

1084 Lincoln Avenue

Do any of these houses look like yours?
Circle the one that looks the most like the house where you live.
Then print your address on the lines below.

"I want to speak to your teacher,"
said the man with the yellow hat.
"Wait for me, George, and don't get into trouble."
You know how to stay out of trouble, and you
can help George. In each of the rows below,
draw a line to the thing that George
can do to stay out of trouble.
With your red crayon, print a big T on
the pictures of George getting into trouble.

Some of the things below belong in school, and
some don't. Color in the things that belong.
Put an X over each thing that doesn't belong.

George was standing in front of the art room.
He opened the door and peeked in.
What did George see when he opened the door?
Color in the correct picture.

Mr. Williams, the art teacher, was cleaning up. Do the crossword puzzle below to find out what Mr. Williams was putting away.

WORD LIST

easel	paper
scissors	paintbrush
crayon	

ACROSS

DOWN

"Hello, George," he said. "My students will be coming by with their parents today to show them their work." You can bring your family to school, too. In the big space below, draw a picture of all the people in your family.

The walls of the art room were covered with the students' paintings.
George likes to paint. Do you?
Draw a line connecting all the things below that you like to do.

13

There were paintings of dancers and farmers
and racing car drivers and ice skaters.
Some of the people in the pictures forgot their shoes.
Draw a line from each person to the right pair of shoes.

What kind of shoes do *you* wear?
Circle all the shoes that are like yours.

On one wall was a chart with the names of all the children.
What are the letters in your name?
Below is the alphabet.
Circle all the letters that are in your name.

ABCDEF
GHIJKL
MNOPQ
RSTUV
WXYZ

Each name had a star beside
it except for Alice's name.
The chart below is *your* chart.
Write in your name.
Then write in the names of three of your friends.
One of your friends already has his name on the chart.
That's right. It's George!

☆	GEORGE
☆	
☆	
☆	
☆	

"Poor Alice," said Mr. Williams.
"She said she left her painting on
my desk, but I can't find it."
Poor Mr. Williams.
Maybe he can't find Alice's painting because he has
things on his desk that don't belong there.
Put an X on everything that doesn't belong.

"Here, George. Why don't you paint a picture while you wait for your friend." The friends below want to play with each other, but they got separated. Draw a line to connect the friends who belong together. Then, draw a picture of yourself with your best friend at the bottom of the page.

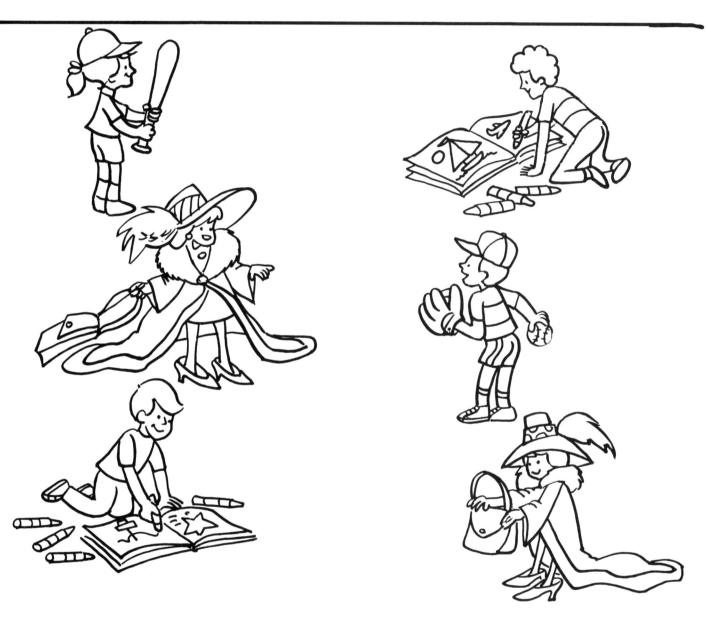

What do *you* like to do when you play? In each row, color in the picture that shows what you would rather do.

On a rainy day, I would rather

read a book.

play a board game with a friend.

On a warm, sunny day, I would rather

ride a bicycle.

wade barefoot in a stream.

On a snowy day, I would rather

build a snowman.

go sledding.

Late at night, I would rather

snuggle up in bed.

go outside and look for stars.

George began to paint.
You can make a picture just like George's.
Color the background blue.
Color the leaves green.
Color the trunk brown.
Color George brown, too.

"Keep painting, George," said Mr. Williams.
"I'll be right back." And off he went.
George didn't finish any of the pictures below.
He forgot how to draw children.
You can finish the pictures for him.

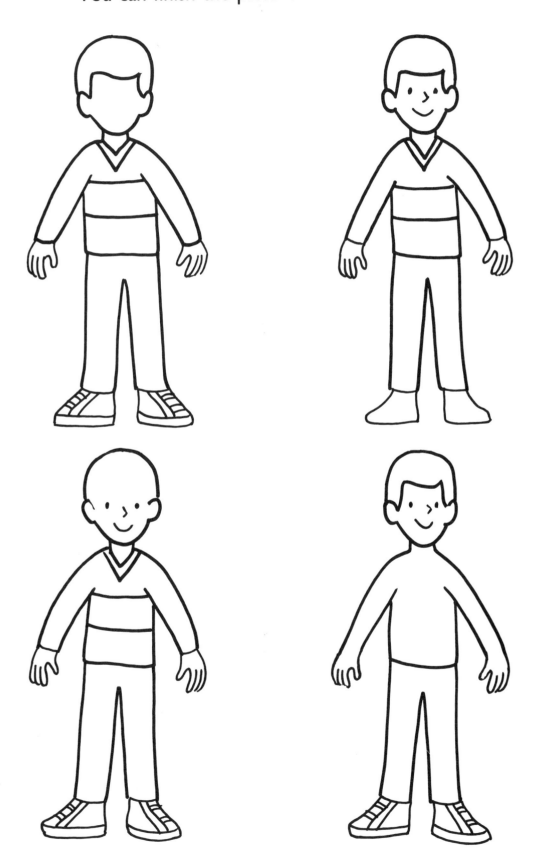

George kept painting. But he had
trouble remembering the names
for different parts of the body.
Do you know them?
Help George by unscrambling the words below.
The numbers below the letters will help you.

m r a

3 2 1

g e f r n i

4 5 1 6 3 2

w o l e b

5 4 2 1 3

e n e k

3 2 4 1

o f t o

3 1 4 2

It was starting to get very warm in the room.
George doesn't wear any clothes, but you do.
What are your favorite clothes?
Draw them here.

On a nearby table sat a big fan.
You can make rhyming words.
The words below rhyme with fan.
Look at each picture and then fill in the
correct letter to complete the word.

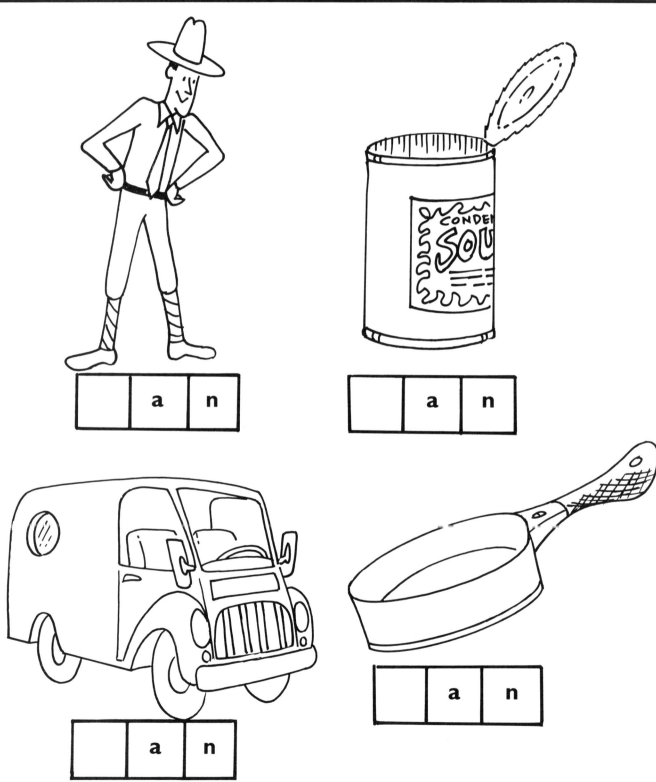

☐ **a n**

☐ **a n**

☐ **a n**

☐ **a n**

That would cool him off!
George turned it on.
Here are some more rhyming words.
In each group, draw a circle around
the two words that rhyme.

But as soon as he did, the fan blew the
paintings off the walls and all over the room!
The pictures below are in the wrong order.
Number them to put them in the right order.

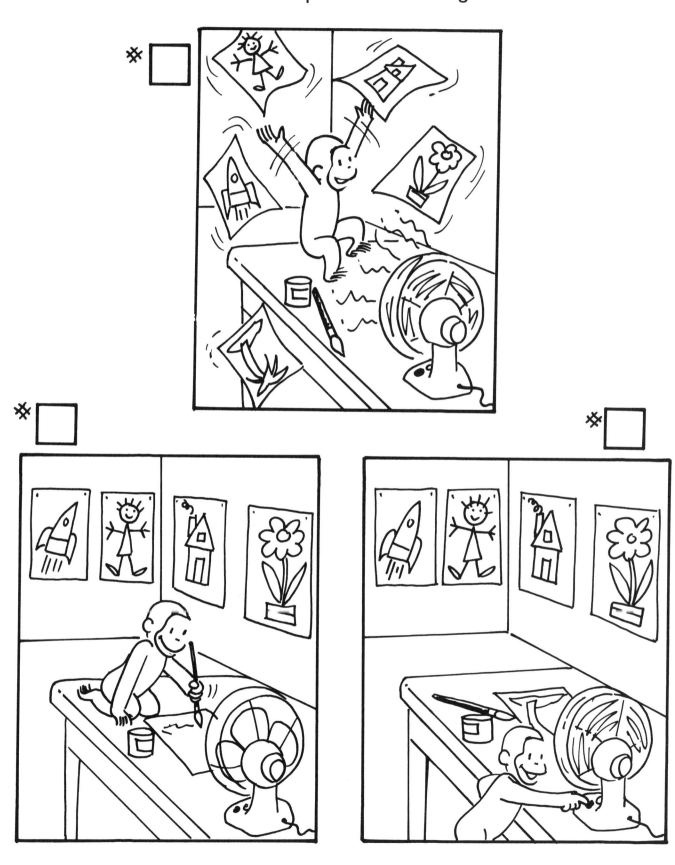

"George!" cried Mr. Williams, running
into the room. "Look what you've done!"
George had been busy making something.
What was it?
To find out, say the word for each picture.
Then print the first letter of each word in the box below the picture.
When the boxes are filled, you will know the answer.

Mr. Williams turned off the fan.

"You'd better help me clean up, George," he said.

These two pictures are not exactly alike.

Draw a circle around the things that are different.

 George doesn't know much about cleaning up, but you do. Draw a line from each thing to the thing that it cleans.

What chores can you help with?
Circle the ones that you are learning.

George picked the papers up off the floor.
George is learning, and you are, too.
Draw a line connecting all the things below
that children can learn to do.

You can do more things now than you could when you
were a baby. Circle the things that babies can do.
Put an X on each thing that babies can't do.

In the art room, some of the papers were under Mr. Williams's desk.
One was stuck between the desk and the wall.
George crawled all over, looking for the papers.
He crawled between the desk and the wall.
Then he climbed over the wastebasket.
Then he crawled under the chair
and ran around the fan.
Draw a line that shows George's path.

When George pulled the paper out, it was covered
with dust, as if it had been there for a long time.
Can your hand fit in a small, tight space?
Spread one of your hands wide
and put it down flat on this piece of paper.
Then trace around your hand and each finger with your crayon.
Now curl your hand up into a tight ball.
Put it down on another part of the paper and trace around it.
Draw a square around the handprint that is bigger.
Circle the handprint that is smaller.

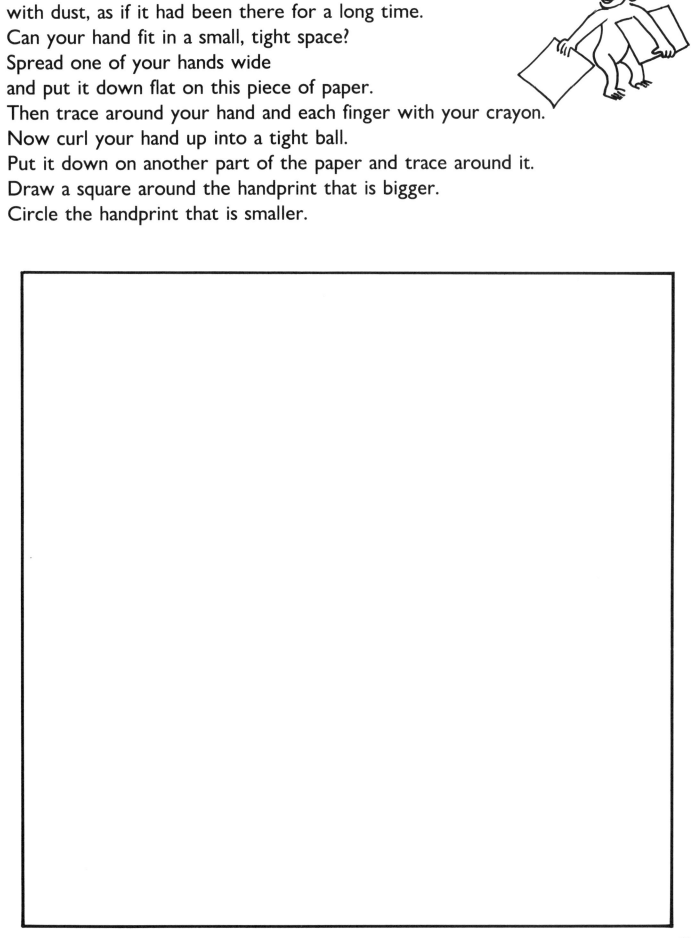

It was a painting of a little girl riding a horse.
Do *you* have any pets?
Draw a circle around the largest pet.
Draw a square around the smallest pet.
Color in the pet that is like yours.
If you don't have a pet,
color in the animal you like best.

Some animals make good pets for
children and some do not.
Would you like the animal below as a pet?
Connect the dots to find out.
Then check one of the boxes below.

YES   NO

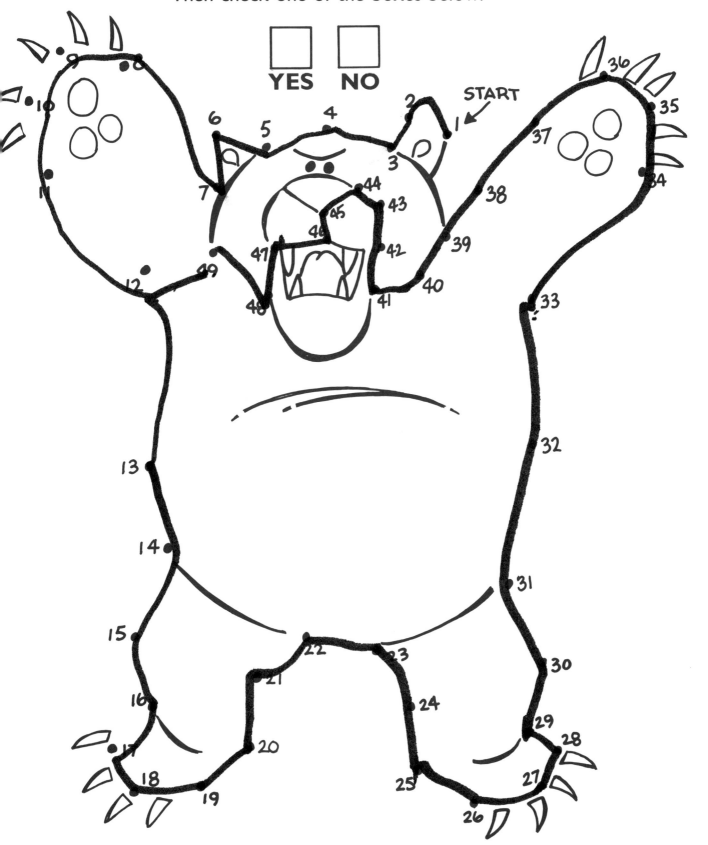

"That's Alice's missing painting!" cried Mr. Williams.
"Now I can give Alice a star."
In each of the pictures below, something is missing.
Draw a line from the missing object
to the picture where it belongs.

KITTY

When the paintings were all hanging on the
walls again, the students and parents arrived.
There are more family members in the
word search puzzle below.
Look across and down. Circle the ones you find.

WORD LIST

mother	grandma
father	grandpa
sister	aunt
brother	uncle
cousin	

```
c z j e p v u f
o g r a n d m a
u n c l e f o t
s b k a u n t h
i y m i w b h e
n b r o t h e r
a s i s t e r x
h g r a n d p a
```

How many people are there in *your* family? _____

There was Alice's painting.
And there was George's painting, right beside it.
In each row, circle the picture that is not like the others.

Now Alice's name on the chart had a gold star next to it.
A star is a shape. Can you draw some other shapes?

○ Draw a circle around the child who is next to the star.
□ Draw a square around the child who is underneath the star.
△ Draw a triangle around the child who is on top of the star.
⬭ Draw a dotted line around the child who is behind the star.

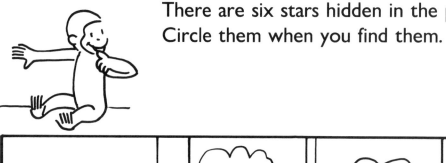

"Thank you for finding my painting, George," said Alice.
"I like your painting, too. You should have a gold star."
There are six stars hidden in the picture below.
Circle them when you find them.

"I agree," said Mr. Williams,
and he gave George a big gold star.
Draw a picture of yourself.
Give yourself a big gold star.

Do you remember the things you read about in this story?
Color in all the pictures below that belong in the story.

☆	George
☆	Susan
☆	Rick
☆	Allen
☆	Alice
☆	Donald

ANSWERS

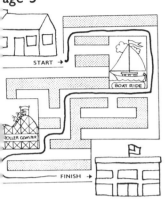

Page 4

like being myself!

Page 5

Page 6

Page 8

Page 9

Page 10

Page 11

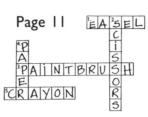

Page 14

Page 18

Page 19

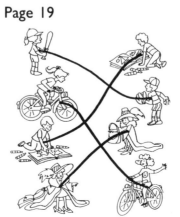

Page 24

Page 26

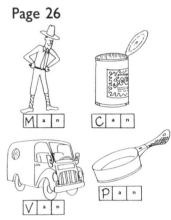

Page 27

Page 28

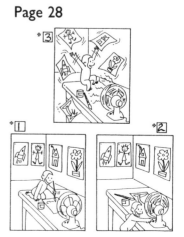

Page 29

A | M E S S

Page 31

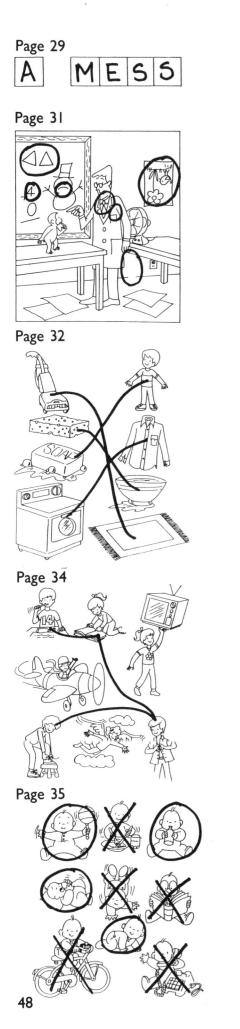

Page 32

Page 34

Page 35

Page 36

Page 38

Page 39

Page 40

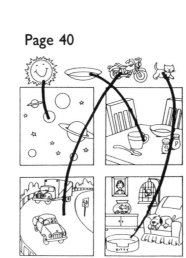

Page 41

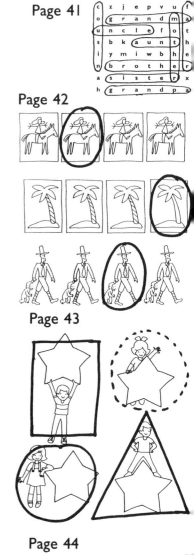

c z j e p v u f
o g r a n d m a
u n c l e f o t
s b k a u n t h
i y m i w b h e
n b r o t h e r
a s i s t e r x
h g r a n d p a

Page 42

Page 43

Page 44

Page 46